Nate the Great
and The
MUSICAL NOTE

For Mom and Dad

with

—C.S.

Published by Yearling, an imprint of Random House Children's Books
a division of Random House, Inc., New York

Yearling and the jumping horse design are registered trademarks of
Random House, Inc.

Visit us on the Web! www.randomhouse.com/kids

**Educators and librarians, for a variety of teaching tools,
visit us at www.randomhouse.com/teachers**

ISBN: 978-0-440-40466-8

Reprinted by arrangement with Putnam & Grosset Book Group,
on behalf of Coward-McCann
Printed in the United States of America
One Previous Edition
New Yearling Edition September 2007
40 39 38

Nate the Great
and The
MUSICAL NOTE

by

Marjorie Weinman Sharmat
and Craig Sharmat

illustrations by Marc Simont

A YEARLING BOOK

I, Nate the Great, am a detective.

This afternoon I was cleaning up
after a big case.

I was sitting in my bathtub singing.

My dog, Sludge, was howling.

I heard a third sound.

The doorbell was ringing.

I stood up.

I rushed toward the door.

I stopped.

I, Nate the Great, was all wet.

I grabbed a towel and my detective hat.

I answered the door.

Pip was there.

"I have come to see you," he said.

Pip's hair covers half his face.

I'm surprised he sees anything.

"Why did you come to see me?" I asked.

Pip didn't answer.

Pip doesn't say much.

"Do you need a detective?" I asked.

"Do you have a case to solve?"

Pip nodded his head

up and down twice.

Then he opened his mouth.

"Right away!" Hurry!" he said.

Pip handed me a piece of paper.

It was a note for Pip from Rosamond.

I knew it would be strange.

I read the note.

"A MUSICAL NOTE FROM ROSAMOND:

Dear Pip,

Your mother phoned.

At four o'clock

when your lesson is through

this is what you have to do:

A note. Step left until

you reach the middle.

Step up and you will

solve this riddle.

Your piano teacher, Rosamond."

I read the note once.

I read the note twice.

I read it three times.

Some things get better with time.

Rosamond's note just got stranger.

I could see why Pip needed me.

"You're taking piano lessons
from Rosamond?" I asked.

Pip nodded his head up and down.

"At Rosamond's house?" I asked.

"At Rosamond's garage," he said.

"I went there to take my lesson.

But I found this note
instead of Rosamond."

"Do you have any idea what
your mother wants you to do

at four o'clock?" I asked.

Pip shrugged.

"Do you know where
your mother is?" I asked.

Pip shrugged again.

"So what does the note mean?" he asked.

"It means that I, Nate the Great,

have a case I must solve

by four o'clock.

It is ten past three.

We don't have much time."

I got dressed fast.

I wrote a quick note to my mother.

Dear Mother,
I am on a case.
I am leaving this note.
It is a much better
note than the one I just
read. I will be back.
Love,
Nate the Great

"We must go to Rosamond's garage,"

I said to Pip.

Pip, Sludge, and I rushed to

Rosamond's garage.

I heard piano music.

I knew we were on the right track.

I rushed into the garage.

I rushed out of the garage.

Annie and her dog, Fang,

were in there,

sitting on a piano bench.

Annie was playing

an old piano.

Fang's mouth was wide open.

He was getting ready to sing.

Or bite.

I didn't want to find out which.

But I had to look for clues.

I went back into the garage

with Pip and Sludge. Slowly.

Annie stopped playing the piano.

Fang closed his mouth.

I was glad about that.

I held up Rosamond's note.

"Do you know anything

about this?" I asked Annie.

"No," Annie said.

"And Rosamond isn't here.

She went out to buy stars."

"Stars?"

"Yes. Rosamond sticks a star on you

if you have a good music lesson.

But now she's late for my lesson.

It was supposed to start at three."

Suddenly Pip spoke.

"Hey, so was mine!" he said.

"Rosamond needs more than stars," I said.

"She needs an appointment book."

I turned to Pip.

"Show me where you found your note."

Pip pointed to the music stand

just above the piano keys.

"Right there," he said.

I looked at the piano.

It was scratched and sagging

and peeling.

But that was not a clue.

I looked around the garage.

In the middle of it I saw
some wide wooden boards
on top of some old blankets.
There was a sign on it.

Rosamond's
STage

It was strange, but it was not a clue.
Or was it?
"Sit down at the piano, Pip,"
I said, "as if you were
taking a lesson from Rosamond."

Annie moved over.

Pip sat down between Annie and Fang.

He was brave.

I, Nate the Great, thought about

where Pip would be if he took

some steps to the left.

He would be in the middle
of the garage.

That fitted with the riddle.

Then if he stepped up,
he would be on Rosamond's stage!

I had solved the case.

It was my easiest case.

Or was it?

Sludge and I sat down on the stage.

I was thinking.

Why would Pip's mother
want him on this stage?

It was full of splinters.

It was not a good place to be.

It couldn't be the answer.

I said, "We will have to wait

for Rosamond to come back

and tell us what the note means."

Pip spoke up.

"I already did that."

"You talk too much," I said.

We all waited.

And waited.

How long could it take

to shop for stars?

Too long.

What if Rosamond didn't come back

until after four o'clock?

Suddenly I saw something shiny.

Rosamond walked into the garage,

carrying a bag full of stars.

She was followed by her four cats,

Super Hex, Big Hex, Plain Hex,

and Little Hex.

They were covered with stars.

I held up Pip's note.

"What does this mean?" I asked.

Rosamond smiled.

"Pip's mother phoned with a message.

I turned it into a music lesson.
Pip has had fifteen minutes
of piano lessons,
so he should know
what my note means.
You're a sharp detective,
so you should also know
what it means."

"I, Nate the Great,

know what this means.

It means I still have a case to solve."

Rosamond grabbed my arm and

pulled me over to the piano.

"How about a piano lesson?" she said.

Pip, Annie, and Fang

got off the bench.

Rosamond sat down.

"I'm going to play the scale

starting from middle C.

Watch my finger

as it moves to the right."

"No," I said. "You watch me

as I move out of this garage.

I am leaving."

Rosamond grabbed my arm again.

"Watch! Middle C.

D. E. F. G. A. B. C."

Rosamond played eight white notes

in a row on her piano.

"I just played a scale

starting with middle C," she said.

"Got it, Nate?"

I, Nate the Great, got it.

But I didn't want it.

I started to sneak out of the garage.

Rosamond kept on.

"See the black notes?

A black note is called a sharp

when it's above a white note,

and it's called

a flat when it's—"

Rosamond stopped talking.

She got up and pulled me back

to the piano.

"I'm not done," she said.

"I gave my cats singing lessons.

Do you want them to know

more than you do?

Do you want them to have
more stars than you?"
"Yes," I said.
Rosamond pressed a white key
near the middle of the keyboard.
I knew it was middle C.
I, Nate the Great, am a fast learner.
Super Hex screeched middle C.
"Very good," Rosamond said.
Sludge did not think so.
He ran out of the garage.

Rosamond moved her finger up
to the black note above middle C.
I knew it was C-sharp.
"This is Big Hex's favorite note,"
she said.
I, Nate the Great, did not want
to hear Big Hex screech C-sharp.
I ran after Sludge.
Pip ran after me.
Rosamond ran after Pip and me.

"You owe me five cents
for the piano lesson,"
she said to me.
Then she reached for Pip.
"It's time for your lesson.
You only have until four o'clock."
Pip turned, took two steps,
and tripped over Sludge.
Rosamond pulled a hairbrush
out of her pocketbook.
She brushed Pip's hair
back from his eyes.
"Now you can see
where you're going," she said.
I said, "I will be back
when I've solved the case."

I turned to Sludge.

"We must look for musical clues.

We have to go where there is music."

Sludge ran ahead.

I knew where he was going.

Five minutes later we were

at the band concert in the park.

Sludge and I sat down under a tree.

"We have to listen hard," I said.

"We have to use our ears and our eyes."

Sludge got up.

He took one step to the left.

He took one step to the right.

He stepped backward and forward.

Sludge was dancing to the music.

Sludge was *not* dancing to the music.

A bee was after Sludge.

I went to rescue him.

Now the bee was after me.

The bee buzzed away.

"Let's go home, Sludge," I said.

I, Nate the Great, needed pancakes.
Pancakes help me think.
Sludge and I started to walk home.
We walked fast.
I only had until four o'clock
to solve this case.
Did I have any good clues?
I had a strange musical note
that told Pip what he had to do
at four o'clock.

But if he did it, he would still be

in Rosamond's garage.

I did not see or hear

any clues in her garage.

All I got was a strange piano lesson.

I did not see or hear any clues

at the band concert.

All I got was a buzzing bee

after Sludge and me.

I kept thinking and walking.

I had to take this case one step at a time.

One step at a time?

I looked at Sludge.

"Sludge, you're a genius.

Your dance steps

that weren't dance steps

at the band concert

have just solved the case."

Sludge and I took giant steps

back to Rosamond's garage.

We stepped inside.

Pip was playing the piano.

Rosamond was leaning over him.

Annie and Fang were watching.

"Stop the music!" I said.

"I, Nate the Great,

have solved your case, Pip.

Please get up, step left to the middle
of the garage, and step up."
Pip followed my directions.
"I'm on the stage!" he said.
"And I, Nate the Great, say
that's where your mother wants
you to be at four o'clock."
"Why?" Pip asked.
I said, "When Sludge and I were
at the concert in the park,
I thought I saw Sludge do dance steps.
That gave me the answer to this case."
"I don't get it," Pip said.
"I will explain," I said.
"Rosamond gives piano lessons
to you and Annie.

Rosamond gives singing lessons
to her cats.
So Rosamond gives different
kinds of lessons."
"So what?" Pip said.
"I, Nate the Great, say that
the steps in Rosamond's note
are a *double* clue.
Ordinary steps
to get to the stage
and dance steps
after you get there.
At four o'clock your mother
wants you to start taking
dancing lessons from Rosamond."
Rosamond clapped her hands.

"That's a wonderful idea.

But it's the wrong answer to this case."

I looked at Sludge.

He wasn't a genius yet.

Maybe later.

"I will be back," I said.

Sludge and I rushed out

of the garage and went home.

It was getting close to four o'clock.

There was time only for quick pancakes.

I gave Sludge a bone.

I had to eat fast

and think faster.

Rosamond said I was a sharp detective.

But this case had fallen

as flat as my pancakes.

Rosamond said that Pip should know

what her note meant

because he had taken piano lessons.

But what about the steps?

I knew they were not

dance steps.

And suddenly I knew more.

Pip was supposed to take the

steps *on the piano!*

I looked at Rosamond's note again.

She had underlined the words "A note."

Why did she underline them?

Because it meant something.

It meant an A note on the piano!

I, Nate the Great, knew

where an A note was.

I, too, had taken a piano lesson

from Rosamond.

I got a piece of paper

and a pencil.

I drew a picture of the piano keys

that Rosamond had used

to play the scale.

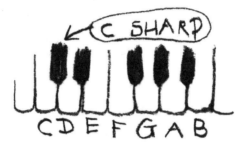

Then I put my finger

on the A note.

I moved my finger

to the left.

I kept going until I reached . . .

middle C!

The middle of the riddle!

So if Pip stepped up from the middle
with his finger, where would he be?
He would be at C-sharp.
Big Hex's favorite note.
The answer to Rosamond's riddle
was C-sharp!
I, Nate the Great, had the answer
to this case at last!
Only one problem was left.
I did not know what the answer meant.

And I had only five minutes left
to find out.

I looked at Sludge.

He was happy eating his bone.

This had not been a good case
for Sludge.

He had almost been stung by a bee.

And Pip had tripped over him.

How could Pip trip over a dog?

Pip's hair covers half his face.

It's hard for him to see anything.

I knew that from the beginning.

But at last I knew it was important!

Sludge had helped with the case

after all.

He had let himself be tripped over.

Sludge and I rushed over

to Rosamond's garage.

We walked in.

Pip was playing the piano.

Rosamond was teaching.

The cats were singing.

I said, "I, Nate the Great,

have solved the case.

The answer to the riddle
is a piano note.
The note is C-sharp.
At four o'clock
Pip is going to *see sharp!*"
Pip spoke up. "What do you mean?"
"You are going to get a haircut,"
I said. "So you will *see sharp*.
Right, Rosamond?"
"Right," Rosamond said.
"Pip's mother said
she is taking him for a haircut.
But I like the idea
of dancing lessons better."
"So do I," Pip said.
"I hate haircuts."

Pip stopped talking.

Pip started running.

Pip started tripping.

He really needed a haircut.

He fell over Super Hex.

Super Hex screeched middle C.

I picked up Pip.

Rosamond picked up Super Hex.

The case was over.

I reached into my pocket,

pulled out five cents,

and gave it to Rosamond.

Then Sludge and I left the garage,

walked to the street, turned,

and started home.

I was singing.

Sludge was howling.

I heard a third sound.

Bells were chiming four o'clock.

~Extra~
Fun Activities!

What's Inside

Middle C.
Sharps and scales.
Pianos are interesting.
Nate wanted to learn more.
He drummed up these facts.

NATE'S NOTES: Pianos

Pianos have eighty-eight keys. Each key connects to a metal string inside the piano. Hit a key and a hammer strikes the string. The string vibrates and makes a sound. The pieces of a piano that move and make music are called the action. A piano has about 7,500 parts.

The first piano was built more than three hundred years ago.

One of the best pianists ever was Mozart. He was born in 1756 and lived in Austria.

Mozart had an amazing life. He began playing short piano pieces at the age of three. At four, he started writing his own music. At five, he was performing for kings and queens. Mozart was like a rock star! He wrote hundreds of pieces of famous music. He died at the age of thirty-five.

Another famous musician who played the piano was Beethoven. He was born in 1770. He lived in Germany and Austria. His father tried to turn Beethoven into a child performer like Mozart. Beethoven didn't learn quite that fast. He was a teenager before he became famous.

By the time Beethoven was forty-nine, he was deaf. He could no longer play the piano. But he kept writing music. Some say the music he wrote when he could no longer hear is his most beautiful.

Player pianos—pianos that play themselves—are neat. An American engineer created the first one in 1897. It was a cabinet with a row of wooden "fingers" that fit over an ordinary piano. Later player pianos "read" rolls of music. The keys moved by themselves. It looked as if a ghost was playing! Player pianos can play music that's impossible for a human. For example, sometimes more than ten keys are played at one time.

Radios and records became popular in the 1930s. They made live music and player pianos less popular. Still, more than 10 million Americans own pianos today.

Piano keys used to be made of ivory. Ivory comes from elephant tusks. In the 1950s, laws were passed to protect elephants. Now piano keys are made of plastic.

The world's largest piano is almost twelve feet long. It is known as the Challen Concert Grand. It was made in England and is said to be housed in a castle somewhere in France.

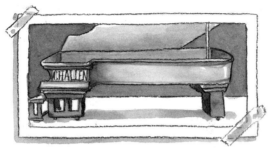

The Yamaha Corporation sells a piano that costs $333,000. It includes a computer and a DVD player. It can re-create piano performances by famous musicians.

NATE'S NOTES: Fingerprints

Nate heard that everyone's fingerprints are different. He decided to learn more. He used the computer at the library and uncovered the following facts.

We leave fingerprints on everything we touch. That makes fingerprints a great way to identify who has been in a certain place. Police often use fingerprints to catch criminals.

People have known that each person's fingerprints are unique since as far back as a thousand years ago.

Police in England began using fingerprints to solve crimes in the 1800s. In America, the FBI began collecting prints in 1920. The FBI now has about 47 million fingerprints on file. (FBI stands for Federal Bureau of Investigation. They solve some very big mysteries.)

Even identical twins have different fingerprints.

Fingerprinting is not an exact science. Our fingerprints are always changing. And prints found at crime scenes are often smudged.

But fingerprints aren't just for solving crimes. Machines can scan your fingerprint and store the picture. Then a scan of your print can be used to open high-tech locks. Some schools even use fingerprint scans in place of library cards.

Humans also have unique toeprints. The FBI does not track these.

Interested in seeing your own fingerprint? It's easy. Press your finger onto an ink pad. Then roll your finger on a piece of white paper. Turn to pages 20 and 21 to learn more.

How to Make Your Own Musical Instrument

Pianos are cool but costly. Another cool instrument is called a rainstick. You can make one at home for about a buck—good for a detective on a budget!

Ask an adult to help you.

GET TOGETHER:

- a cardboard tube. Try a mailing tube, a paper towel roll, or even a toilet paper tube. Any size will work.

- about four dozen nails (more for a big tube). The nails should be about half as long as the distance across your tube. It's okay if they're longer, but they shouldn't be long enough to poke through the other side.
- a hammer, if you're using a thick tube like a mailing tube
- end caps for the tube OR a piece of construction paper, a pencil, and scissors
- colorful masking tape
- 1 cup of rice, lentils, or dried beans

MAKE YOUR RAINSTICK:

1. Hammer the nails into the tube. If your tube is small, you can push the nails in without a hammer. Just be sure that the nails are more or less evenly spaced.

2. Close up one end of the tube. Use a cap if you have one. If not, trace one end of the tube onto construction paper. Cut out the circle. Tape it in place.

3. Pour the rice, lentils, or beans into the tube.

4. Close up the other end of the tube.

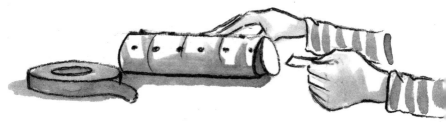

5. Use the masking tape to decorate the tube. This will also help hold the nails in place. Cover the ends with tape, too.

6. To play your new instrument, slowly turn it over. You should hear the sound of rain falling.

The people of Mexico have made rainsticks for many years. The idea may have originally come from Africa.

Funny Pages

Q: Why did the piano player keep hitting the keys with the side of his head?
A: *He was playing by ear.*

Q: What's the difference between a piano and a tuna fish?
A: *You can't tuna fish.*
A: *Sure you can! Just adjust its scales.*

Man 1: I've come to tune your piano.

Man 2: I didn't call you.

Man 1: I know. Your next-door neighbor did.

The piano is more than three hundred years old. So is the statement "But I don't WANT to practice."

How to Lift a Fingerprint

People never stop leaving their fingerprints behind. If you try, you can pick up, or "lift," someone's prints. Use the following tips.

Ask an adult to help you.

GET TOGETHER:

- a paintbrush
- a piece of charcoal
- clear tape
- white paper

CAPTURE A FINGERPRINT:

1. "Paint" the charcoal until your paintbrush is covered with black dust.

2. Gently brush the dust onto a surface where you think there may be fingerprints. HINT: Fingerprints are easiest to lift off hard, smooth surfaces. Try a drinking glass, a doorknob, or the cookie jar.

3. Press a piece of clear tape on top of any prints you see.

4. Stick the tape onto white paper. You've just "lifted" a fingerprint!

5. Don't forget to clean any areas you've dusted.

Using an ink pad, collect fingerprint samples from your family and other people who spend time at your house. Then you can compare your "lifted" fingerprints with the samples.

Having a hard time finding fingerprints? Try putting a few of your own prints on a glass. Sticky or oily fingers leave the best prints.

Three Types of Fingerprints

Each fingerprint is different, but there are three main types of fingerprint patterns.

An **arch** is formed by lines running from one side of the finger to the other. The lines curve up in the middle.

A **loop** has a steeper curve than an arch. The lines begin and end on the same side.

A **whorl** is a spiral pattern with one dot in the center.

Some fingerprints, though, don't fit any of these three patterns:

A **composite print** is one that mixes two of the main types, like a whorl and a loop.

An **accidental print** is one that's too weird to fit into any of the main types. It might look like a squashed whorl or have extra dots. There aren't many of these.

More Funny Pages

Knock, knock.
Who's there?
Stopwatch.
Stopwatch who?
Stop watch you're doing right now!

Q: What's up a clean nose?
A: Fingerprints!

Q: Why isn't Fang a good dancer?
A: *Because he has two left feet!*

Q: Where do fortune-tellers dance?
A: *At the crystal ball.*

Q: What is a pig's favorite ballet?
A: *Swine Lake!*

Q: Where did the spaghetti go to dance?
A: *The meatball.*

Q: Where did the computer go to dance?
A: *The disc-o!*

Q: What kind of dance do you do in the sink?
A: *A tap dance!*

Q: Why was the ballerina a great debater?
A: *She always got right to the pointe.*

Q: Where do you go to learn how to belly dance?
A: *The navel academy!*

Q: How do belly dancers keep their costumes together?
A: *With belly buttons.*

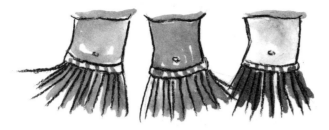

Q: What kind of music do frogs like?
A: *Hip-hop!*

Q: What's a geologist's favorite kind of music?
A: *Rock!*

Q: What do you call a car with music coming out of it?
A: *A car-toon!*

Q: What's green and sings?
A: *Elvis Parsley!*

Have you helped solve all Nate the Great's mysteries?

❑ **Nate the Great**: Meet Nate, the great detective, and join him as he uses incredible sleuthing skills to solve his first big case.

❑ **Nate the Great Goes Undercover**: Who— or what—is raiding Oliver's trash every night? Nate bravely hides out in his friend's garbage can to catch the smelly crook.

❑ **Nate the Great and the Lost List**: Nate loves pancakes, but who ever heard of cats eating them? Is a strange recipe at the heart of this mystery?

❑ **Nate the Great and the Phony Clue**: Against ferocious cats, hostile adversaries, and a sly phony clue, Nate struggles to prove that he's still the world's greatest detective.

❑ **Nate the Great and the Sticky Case**: Nate is stuck with his stickiest case yet as he hunts for his friend Claude's valuable stegosaurus stamp.

❑ **Nate the Great and the Missing Key**: Nate isn't afraid to look anywhere—even under the nose of his friend's ferocious dog, Fang—to solve the case of the missing key.